WHERE'S THE PRINCESS?

AND OTHER FAIRY TALE SEARCHES

There are things to spot in every scene in this magical book—from Cinderella's lost slipper to Aladdin's magic lamp. If you get stuck, all the answers are in the back.

I'm also hidden in every scene— can you find me?

Chuck Whelon

ALADDIN

NEW YORK   LONDON   TORONTO   SYDNEY   NEW DELHI

Little Red Riding Hood

1 Little Red Riding Hood

1 daffodil

1 basket

1 nest

1 strawberry plant

5 toadstools

1 bear

4 orange butterflies

7 acorns

1 Big Bad Wolf

2 deer

Cinderella

1 prince

6 footmen

1 wicked stepmother

1 glass slipper

6 mice

3 pumpkins

1 Cinderella

1 fairy

2 mean sisters

4 bats

1 clock

The Little Mermaid

1 Sea King

7 seahorses

1 oyster shell and pearl

1 red-and-yellow fish

3 starfish

1 anchor

1 dolphin

1 weeping willow tree

1 marble statue

5 jellyfish

1 Little Mermaid

Snow White

1
Snow
White

7
dwarves

3 squirrels

1 roast chicken

7 pickaxes

7 little loaves of bread

1 wicked witch

1 little lamps

1 red robin

2 rabbits

1 big polka-dot pot

Sleeping Beauty

1 kind fairy

3 sleeping violinists

1 wicked fairy

1 golden eagle

1 Sleeping Beauty

2 sleeping dogs

1 prince

5 sleeping guards

1 sleeping queen

1 sleeping king

1 spinning wheel

The Princess and the Pea

7 maids

1 prince

5 chairs

1 pea

1 crown in a painting

1 polka-dot blanket

3 striped cushions

1 bowl of fruit

1 goofy portrait

1 queen

1 long ladder

Hansel and Gretel

1 Hansel

1 Gretel

3 owls

1 mouse

1 snow-white bird

10 candy canes

5 gingerbread men

1 witch

3 mallard ducks

2 rabbits

1 wishing well

The Pied Piper of Hamelin

1 Pied Piper

1 minstrel

1 horse

1 man in the stockade

2 wheelbarrows

1 cat and her kittens

1 man falling off a ladder

1 woman

1 basket of laundry

2 children dancing

1 rat on a clothesline

1 genie

1 princess

5 bats

1 lamp

1 ruby tiara

4 blue goblets

1 Aladdin

1 jeweled necklace

1 chest of gold coins

1 golden camel

The Frog Prince

1 golden ball

1 queen

3 spotted lily pads

4 dragonflies

3 mallard
ducks

5 rosebushes

1
golden
boy

1
princess

6 pond
snails

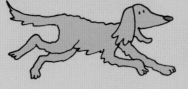

1 dog

1 Frog Prince

Jack and the Beanstalk

1 Jack

1 Jack's mother

1 Daisy the cow

10 gold coins

3 sheep

5 snakes

1 gold harp

1 giant

1 ax

3 ladybugs

1 hen with a golden egg

Pinocchio

1 jack-in-the-box

1 Pinocchio

1 wooden doll

2 pairs of wooden shoes

5 hammers

4 jars of paint

1 Geppetto

1 cuckoo clock

1 wind-up ballerina

3 spinning tops

1 sly fox and cat

1 rocking horse

Answers

Cinderella

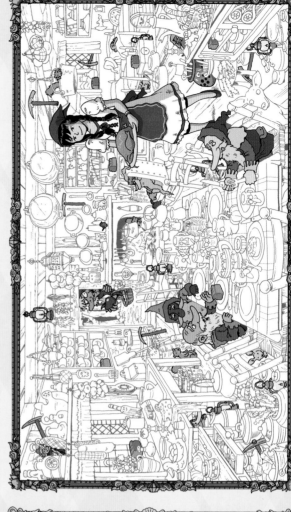

Snow White

Little Red Riding Hood

The Little Mermaid

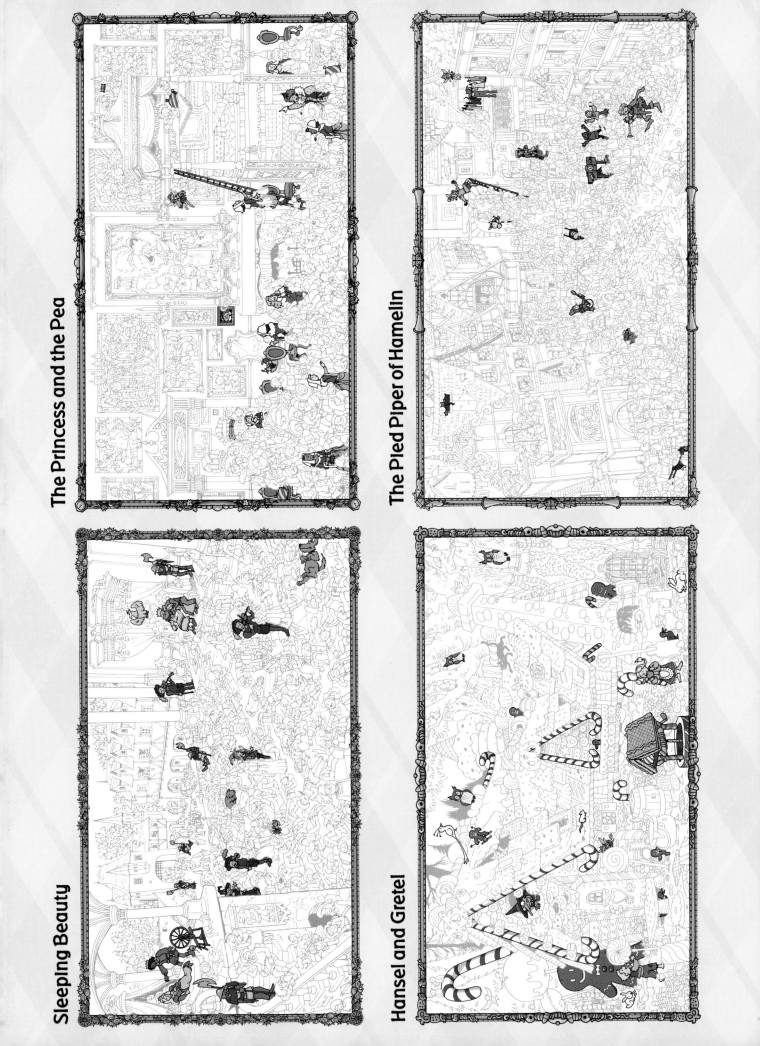

The Princess and the Pea

The Pied Piper of Hamelin

Sleeping Beauty

Hansel and Gretel

Answers

The Frog Prince

The Adventures of Aladdin

Pinocchio

Jack and the Beanstalk

ALADDIN
An imprint of Simon & Schuster Children's Publishing Division
1230 Avenue of the Americas, New York, NY 10020
This Aladdin hardcover edition February 2016
Copyright © 2014 by Buster Books
Originally published as *The Great Fairy Tale Search* in 2014 in Great Britain by Buster Books.
All rights reserved, including the right of reproduction in whole or in part in any form.
ALADDIN is a trademark of Simon & Schuster, Inc., and related logo is a registered trademark of Simon & Schuster, Inc.
For information about special discounts for bulk purchases, please contact
Simon & Schuster Special Sales at 1-866-506-1949 or business@simonandschuster.com.
The Simon & Schuster Speakers Bureau can bring authors to your live event. For more information or to book an event
contact the Simon & Schuster Speakers Bureau at 1-866-248-3049 or visit our website at www.simonspeakers.com.
Designed by Karina Granda
The text for this book was set in Interstate.
Manufactured in China 1019 SCP
4 6 8 10 9 7 5
Library of Congress Control Number 2015938952
ISBN 978-1-4814-4633-4 (POB)